POCKET
HEROES

ROBIN HOODiE

SWEETS

MORE SWEETS

DAVE WOODS
CHRIS INNS

ORCHARD

As most folk know, Robin Hood was a legendary outlaw. He was also known as the Hooded Man. But before he was a man, he was a boy (with a hood).

Yes, he was Robin Hoodie!

A long, long time ago, England was covered in forests. (More forests than you could shake a stick at.)

New forests and ancient forests and short forests and tall forests and bald forests and even haunted forests (full of petrified wood).

ROBIN HOODIE

For Nic and Adrian
C.I.

For Maureen, Jo, Paul, Daniel & Neve –
my support team in the Shire
D.W.

ORCHARD BOOKS
338 Euston Road, London NW1 3BH
Orchard Books Australia
Level 17/207 Kent Street, Sydney, NSW 2000

First published in 2013
First paperback publication in 2014

ISBN 978 1 40831 358 9 (hardback)
ISBN 978 1 40831 364 0 (paperback)

A CIP catalogue record for this book is available
from the British Library.

1 3 5 7 9 10 8 6 4 2 (hardback)
1 3 5 7 9 10 8 6 4 2 (paperback)

Printed in Great Britain

Orchard Books is a division of Hachette Children's Books,
an Hachette UK company.

www.hachette.co.uk

But the most famous forest of all...
was Sherbet Forest!

Today, in Sherbet Forest, was
market day at YE OLDE LOOWATER
SHOPPING CENTRE.

There were farmers selling crops, butchers selling chops, cleaners selling mops, brewers selling hops and barbers trimming fops.

WH Blacksmiths was selling pens. (Chicken pens, sheep pens, cattle pens and pig pens.)

The Gap between some trees was displaying tunics, tabards and other garments (in any colour you like, as long as it's green).

Roots the Chemist had a special on dog-cleaning products – buy one get one flea.

And some Watery Stones led to
a bookshop on the other side of the
pond...

The village idiot had even tried to
open a paper shop, but it blew away.

Yes, YE OLDE LOOWATER
SHOPPING CENTRE had everything.
Well, almost...

"WHERE ARE THE SWEETS?" cried Ivan Hoe, the tool seller. He was part of a large crowd that had gathered around the empty sweet stall.

"THEY'VE BEEN TAKEN BY ROTTERS!" said Beatrix the potter.

Yes, the sherbet dib-dabs had been nib-nabbed…

The pick 'n' mix had been pick 'n' nicked...

Chocolate coins had been pocketed...

Lemon bon-bons had gone-gone...

(You get the idea.)

Who had grabbed THE GOODIES?

THE BADDIES, of course!

The baddies were Naughty Prince Johnny and the Short Sheriff of Nuttingham.

For years, these two rich kids had put a SWEET TAX on the poor children of England!

More and more sweets were swiped. Until, finally…

All the goodies were gone!

The poor children were miserable. Sisters were sad. Brothers were grim.

"We've been robbed of our childhoods!" wept the slaughterman's daughter.

"Without sweets, we're stuffed!" cried the stonemason's son.

Yes, the SWEET TAX was as bad as taking candy from a baby.

(Hang on, it *was* taking candy from babies!)

Suddenly, there came a voice from (low down) in the crowd…

GOOD FOLK OF SHERBET FOREST, LISTEN, I CAN HELP THEE…

The crowd looked up – and saw no one.

So the crowd looked down – and saw…

A Robin.

Not a Robin with a bright red breast and a beak.

No.

A Robin with a
Lincoln Green shirt and
a hood.
A boy.

A Hooded Boy! With a shortbow in
his hand, a glint in his eye and an idea
in his head.

It was Robin Hoodie!

"'TIS I, ROBIN HOODIE!" he said.

(See, told you it was him.)

"How can you help?" demanded Sid Viscous, the treacle trader.

"I HAVE A SWEET IDEA!" said Robin Hoodie, bravely.

"Spit it out," urged Jenny Rotten, the fruit seller.

"WE MUST TAKE SWEETS BACK FROM THOSE TWO RICH KIDS TO GIVE TO THE POOR KIDS!"

The crowd fell silent.

"'Ow much will this fancy idea of yours cost us, then?" asked Johnny Debt, the moneylender.

"'TIS FREE!" replied Robin Hoodie, nobly. "All I need is a band of you to help me…"

"TAKE YOUR PICK!" shouted the boys, merrily.

So he did.

I need to find a band of boys, To help me make a bit of noise. Make 'em smart, make 'em scary, But most of all, make 'em Mer-ry!

WILL STARLETT

*Flashing smile and flashing blade,
A dandy of the forest glade!*

ELEANOR DALE

*Our minstrel here plays rough & tumble,
A real tomboy – she loves to rumble!*

SNOOP FROGGY FROG

In dancin' terms,
he's one-in-a-million,
Hip-hoppin', hip-skippin',
hip-jumpin' amphibian!

A word on the rappin'
of Robin Hoodie:
We wish we could
say at least
somethin' goodie,
But his rhymes are lousy
and his rap is bad,
When he's finished these
intros we'll be
mighty glad!

23

And so it was that Robin Hoodie
and his Merry Boyz went looking for
action and adventure. Or adventure and
action. (They weren't fussy – either way,
they were on a mission!)

The next morning, the Merry Boyz
positioned themselves in the treetops,
waiting for their first chance to grab
back some goodies for the poor kids.

It looked like their luck was in!
One of the wealthy-looking carriages
from Nuttingham Castle sped through
Sherbet Forest. And tied to the back of
the carriage was a huge sack.

"Aha!" cried Robin Hoodie. "More
goodies being taken back to Naughty
Prince Johnny!"

The Merry Boyz dropped from the
oak trees like acorns in a storm. They
surrounded the carriage.

"Stand and deliver…your sweets!" demanded Robin Hoodie.

But instead of an armful – all he got was a mouthful (and not of goodies).

"I HAVEN'T GOT ANY SWEETS!" cried a little, girly voice from within the carriage.

Robin Hoodie was surprised. "Come down from the carriage," he demanded.

When the little, girly voice came down from the carriage, it belonged to (surprise, surprise) a little girl.

"Who are you?" asked Robin Hoodie (valiantly).

"I'm MAID MARIONETTE!" said Maid Marionette.

"What's in the sack, then?" asked Robin.

"Oh, that. Well, the rich kids at Nuttingham Castle are always eating sweets…so I popped down to YE OLDE LOOWATER SHOPPING CENTRE to get them their 'five a day'."

"'Tis true, Robin," said Friar Tuckshop, pulling open the sack and revealing a (healthy-looking) variety of fruit and veg.

"You're bananas," said Robin to Maid Marionette.

"And you're a lemon," she replied (sourly).

But Robin Hoodie (who knew his onions) had an idea!

"In that case…" said Robin to Maid Marionette, "we'll kidney bean you!"

"Er, don't you mean kidnap me?" said Maid Marionette.

"Exactly!" said Robin. "We'll kidnap you…for a sweet ransom!"

And so the Merry Boyz kidnapped
Maid Marionette and took her to their
EVER-SO-SECRET HOODIE HIDEOUT.
(Which was ever-so, ever-so secret
indeed.)

"I've got Marionette for ransom,
Plus her carriage and her horse.
She'll be swapped for
golden coins
(made from chocolate,
of course!)."

scribble
scritch
scratch
scribble
scribble

Hear that sound? It's Robin Hoodie, writing the ransom note in the dead of night! Shhh!

The next morning, Robin awoke. "I've slept like a log!" he yawned. (That's what happens when you're surrounded by leaves and branches and trunks and trees…)

After breakfast, Maid Marionette asked Robin Hoodie why he and the Merry Boyz were baddies.

"We're not baddies," said Robin Hoodie, "we're goodies!"

He explained how the rich kids – Naughty Prince Johnny and the Short Sheriff of Nuttingham – had been taking sweets from the poor children.

"Goodies gracious me!" exclaimed Maid Marionette. "I never realised Naughty Prince Johnny was so, um… naughty!"

"We've even got a ballad about him!" added Eleanor Dale.

(A 'ballad' is an olde word for a song.)

*"Sweet England is ruled
by a sour-faced villain,
He's spiteful and mean
and very uncouth.
Yes, the only sweet thing about
Naughty Prince Johnny
Is that Naughty Prince Johnny
has got a sweet tooth!"*

"I see…" nodded Maid Marionette.
"You're good baddies…that grab back
goodies…from bad goodies!"

"Er…exactly," said Robin Hoodie.

"Well, let me help you!" Maid Marionette offered.

Robin Hoodie stood up. (He liked to think on his feet.) He screwed up the ransom note. Then they all huddled around the campfire and made...

A new plan.

THE NEW PLAN involved...a bush.

Can you guess what sort of bush?

A holly bush?
No.

A mulberry bush?
No.

A Shepherd's Bush?

No.

It was the Merry Boyz's favourite kind of bush...

An am-bush!

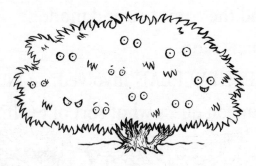

(You see, because Maid Marionette lived in Nuttingham Castle, she knew exactly when Naughty Prince Johnny would travel through Sherbet Forest. And the next time he did... Well... shhh... Keep reading...)

A few days later, the Merry Boyz were waiting quietly, when...

The most princely carriage they'd ever seen appeared. (Well, it did belong to a prince.) Inside were Naughty Prince Johnny and the Short Sheriff of Nuttingham.

The Merry Boyz sprang into action!

"Stand and deliver...your sweets!" they said (confidently).

But the sweet chariot drove straight past!

"Ah," they said.

Suddenly, though, the carriage screeched to a halt. Robin Hoodie was standing in front of it – with a grin on his face and a carrot in his hand.

"To stop a carriage…" he said, "…you must first stop the horse!"

(Which, frankly, you can't argue with.)

Inside the carriage, the two baddies were hiding under their seats. And listening. (But mostly, they were hiding under their seats.)

"It's that outlaw, Robin Hoodie!" whispered the Short Sheriff.

"Where are my guards?" asked Naughty Prince Johnny.

"Sire, you said stuff the carriage with as many sweets as possible."

"I did?"

"You did, Sire. So I replaced the guardies…with goodies."

"You did?"

"I did, Sire."

"Sugar!" said Naughty Prince Johnny.

"HAND OVER THE BON-BONS!" commanded Robin Hoodie. "CHOP-CHOP!"

The baddies were bullies. But without their big, tough guards to protect them…they were sissies. (All bullies are like this.)

"Very well," they whimpered. "You win!"

(See.)

Naughty Prince Johnny jumped from the carriage, but couldn't resist one final boast...

"Keep your carriage of sweets, you do-goodie Hoodie! They're a pear drop in the ocean compared to the tower full of sweets I have in Nuttingham Castle! Hah!"

With that, the little losers legged it.

Hmmm…thought Robin Hoodie – he could feel a rap coming on…

> *Those boastful baddies*
> *haven't got us beat,*
> *I've just had a plan*
> *that's twice as…sweet!*

> *Your rhymes are rubbish*
> *And your raps are bad,*
> *You're no Eminem,*
> *You're a Nottingham Lad!*

Early the next morning, Robin Hoodie, Maid Marionette and the Merry Boyz left Sherbet Forest. (They weren't satisfied with just a carriage-full of sweets – they wanted the whole tower-full!) They travelled light, carrying some large, folded-up sacks, a musical instrument, one clever disguise…and one (even more clever) plan.

They arrived at Nuttingham Castle.

(They say 'An Englishman's home is his castle'. In Naughty Prince Johnny's case, his home *was* a castle!)

Once inside, they huddled.

"Time to put my plan into action," whispered Robin Hoodie.

First, the Merry Boyz disappeared into the crowd.

RUMBLE BUBBLE

Then, Maid Marionette vanished
behind a hut (which served pizza – Ham
& Crab-apple was their bestseller).

Seconds later, a wandering musician
appeared from behind the hut –
complete with beard and moustache…

And a lute.

(A lute is a fancy medieval word for
a guitar.)

The musician (look closely, you'll recognise 'him') headed toward some heavy oak doors.

"What do you want, musician?" grunted the door guard.

"I have a ballad to sing for Nice Prince Johnny."

"You mean Naughty Prince Johnny?" said the guard.

"Go tell him he's Naughty not Nice…" said the musician. "I dare thee!"

And you know what?

The guard didn't dare.

"Er, you better enter," said the confused guard.

(And while the guard was distracted, in crept the Merry Boyz...)

Seated next to a window, Naughty Prince Johnny and the Short Sheriff were busy counting their lollies.

Naughty Prince Johnny:
"*A lolly for me (crunch, crunch),*
a stick for you...
A lolly for me (crunch, crunch),
a stick for you..."
Out of the window behind them towered the tall sweet tower.

"Sire," interrupted the guard. "This musician has a ballad for thee."

"Me?" said Naughty Prince Johnny. "Why?"

"Because you are the sweetest prince in the land," lied the musician.

"I am?"

The Short Sheriff nudged him with his elbow.

"Er, yes, I AM!" corrected Naughty Prince Johnny. "MUSICIAN, SING!"

*Fair England is ruled by a
sweet-hearted hero,
Who's helpful and brave and
fights for the truth.
And the other sweet thing about
Nice Prince Johnny
Is that Nice Prince Johnny
has got a sweet tooth!*

"Encore!" giggled Naughty
Prince Johnny.

('Encore' is a fancy French word for
'play it again'.)

So Maid Marionette did.

And while she was busy singing…

And Naughty Prince Johnny was
busy listening…

The Merry Boyz were…gone!

Robin Hoodie and the Merry Boyz had sneaked around to the sweet tower.

"It's too tall!' said Very Littlejohn (who knew a thing or two about being tall).

"No," grinned Robin Hoodie, "it's just the right height…" He pulled out his shortbow and notched a sucker arrow, "…FOR A LADDER!"

He fired a whole quiver of arrows at the sweet tower.

(Sucker arrows – marvellous, aren't they?)

Up climbed the Merry Boyz. Very Littlejohn used his very big muscles to pull open the window bars – and inside was a treasure trove of goodies!

(The Merry Boyz were like kids in a sweet shop.)

Robin Hoodie handed out the sacks. "Fill 'em up, Merry Boyz!"

So they stuffed the sacks with sweets and crammed them with caramels, until they were bulging with bon-bons and chocka with chocolate. Then they tiptoed back down the arrow staircase.

Maid Marionette was waiting for them.

"Nice looting!" she said, looking at Robin Hoodie's loot.

"Nice lute-ing!" said Robin Hoodie, looking at Marion's lute.

"Never mind the loot," shouted Friar Tuckshop. "It's time to scoot!"

Running towards them were (in alphabetical order!):

An **A**ngry army of guards…

A **B**ad-tempered
Naughty Prince
Johnny…

A **C**ross Short
Sheriff
of Nuttingham!

(**D**on't just stand there, Robin Hoodie… **E**scape!)

Robin Hoodie and the Band of Merry Boyz tried to escape through the gates of Nuttingham Castle, but there was a problem…

"Where's the BRIDGE?" cried Maid Marionette.

"We have to DRAW it," explained Robin Hoodie.

"Why?"

"Because it's A DRAWBRIDGE!"

(Obvious, really.)

Robin Hoodie pulled a set of (quill) pens from his quiver and drew a large, wooden bridge.

They all ran across it.

"Now," grinned Robin Hoodie, "we do this…"

(You see, Robin Hoodie wasn't just good with robbers…he was good with rubbers, too.)

But Maid Marionette was still worried. "What if they try and swim across the moat?"

Robin Hoodie handed her the quill pens – he could feel another rap coming on…

(Unfortunately.)

*"The guards are coming
so keep me happy,
Sketch a big croc –
and make it snappy!"*

And with that, the Merry Boyz
headed off to the safety of Sherbet
Forest.

The next day was MAY DAY!
(This is when children celebrate the
arrival of spring.)

But on this May Day, the poor kids of Sherbet Forest celebrated the arrival of something different.

For every child found a bag on their doorstep.

And each bag was overflowing with sweets – of every flavour you could imagine! Plus a nice piece of cake, a few puzzles...and a plastic whistle.

(Delivered by young Robin himself... they were 'Hoodie Bags'!)

"Your Merry Boyz are midget gems,
They showed those baddies proppa.
But Hooded Boy, your rap's so bad
Your gift's a big gobstoppa!"

Our hero was speechless – for now.

And what became of Robin Hoodie?
Well, that's another story…

DAVE WOODS
CHRIS INNS

SHORT JOHN SILVER	978 1 40831 359 6
SIR LANCE-A-LITTLE	978 1 40831 360 2
ROBIN HOODIE	978 1 40831 364 0
JUNIOR CAESAR	978 1 40831 362 6
FLORENCE NIGHTINGIRL	978 1 40831 363 3
HENRY THE 1/8TH	978 1 40831 361 9

All softbacks priced at £4.99

Orchard Books are available from all good bookshops,
or can be ordered from our website: www.orchardbooks.co.uk,
or telephone 01235 827702, or fax 01235 827703.